THE DAY THE COW

SNEEZED

THE DAY THE

COW SNEEZED

Story and Pictures by

JAMES FLORA

Enchanted Lion Books
New York

FOR CAROLINE FLORA
An early-mooing non-sneezer

www.enchantedlionbooks.com

Published in 2010 by Enchanted Lion Books
20 Jay Street, Studio M-18, Brooklyn, NY 11201
Originally published in 1957 by Harcourt, Brace & World, Inc. © by James Flora, 1957
All rights reserved under International and Pan-American Copyright Conventions
ISBN 978-1-59270-097-4

Digital art restoration: Barbara Economon
Solicitor and Overseer: Irwin Chusid
Designer: Laura Lindgren
Printed in July 2010 in China by South China Printing Co.Ltd

’ll bet your cow never sneezed a hole in the school-house wall. Our cow did. Our old cow Floss sneezed so hard that she tore down the city hall, opened up the zoo, and scared the whole city of Sassafras Springs. All with one sneeze.

Of course it wasn't really old Floss's fault that she sneezed so hard. My brother Fletcher is the one to blame.

Every morning before he goes to school, Fletcher takes our cow Floss down to the creek for a drink of water. One morning while old Floss was drinking, my brother Fletcher spied a little rabbit hopping across the pasture. He always wanted a pet rabbit, so he lit out after him. He chased it at least a mile, but he couldn't catch it because even a baby rabbit can run faster than a boy.

While he was gone, Floss drank too much water, and she got chilled standing in the cold creek. When Fletcher put her back in the barn, she was shaking and shivering.

She was shaking so much she could barely eat her morning hay. Her nose got redder and redder and began to itch. Her eyes watered. Her throat tickled. "K-k-k-k—"

"KA-CHOW" she sneezed.

A mouse was sleeping in Floss's hay. That powerful sneeze blew him right out of bed.

The cat saw the mouse,
leaped at it, missed,
and landed on the billy goat.

When the billy goat felt the cat clawing
at his back, he raced out of the barn and
down the road in a fearful fright.

BAM! He bowled over the pig.

POW! He knocked down the mailman and the mailbox too.

CRASH! He bashed into a motorcycle policeman. The policeman fell off, and the billy goat landed on the motorcycle.

Down the road they flew, over the bridge,
up the hill, through the woods, and over the
cliff by Jack Makemson's barn.

They fell with a flip-flop and a loop-the-loop
and landed on a steam roller.

Now, everyone knows that a billy goat
doesn't know how to drive a steam roller.
Neither does a cat, nor a mouse for that matter.
So the steam roller was able to go wherever it
wanted, and away it went at full speed.

First it flattened a few trees. Then it mashed a street
lamp, a fireplug, and a laundry truck. The mayor and
the policemen tried to stop it, but they couldn't catch it.

The steam roller charged right on through the park
and picked up a statue and a cannon. It knocked over
City Hall and two stores. Then it tore right through the
schoolhouse wall.

Fletcher was reciting in social studies, and when he saw our cat and our billy goat on the steam roller, he jumped on too and tried to stop it. But he couldn't find the right lever.

CRASH! They went through the other wall of the school and ripped down the street.

BING! BANG! SMASH! TINKLE!

Iron deer, picket fences, trains, gas stations, ice cream trucks—everything was scrunched as flat as corn flakes.

KA-BLOWIE-BLAM!

They ripped through the fence around the zoo.

My, what a mess! They broke the cages, right and left, freeing all the animals. The elephant tried to stop the roller, but the roller was too strong, and it really changed the look of that elephant. In fact, the roller changed the looks of just about every animal in the zoo.

It put a zigzag
in the giraffe's neck.
Flattened the moose's horns.

Pressed a large alligator.

Bent the rhino's snout.

Curlicued the octopus.

Made a crinkly lion and
flattened a fat elephant.

All the other animals jumped on top of the steam roller
as fast as they could. It was the only safe place to be.

"STOP!" everyone was shouting.

But the steam roller kept right on at full speed.

It ran through the pond in the park and changed all
of the fish. It mashed a tree and changed a few birds.
Then it started for the merry-go-round.

WHAMBO! It missed the merry-go-round but crashed into the big Ferris wheel. All the animals and my brother Fletcher jumped and clutched at the seats of the big wheel.

They were happy to leave that crazy steam roller. They thought they were safe and sound, but the steam roller had knocked the big Ferris wheel off its base, and it started to roll away.

"WHOA-A-A!" shouted Fletcher, but the wheel was rolling so fast nobody could hold it. It ran over the popcorn, peanut, cotton candy, and lemonade stands, and food flew everywhere. At least they wouldn't be hungry.

POPCORN

ICE CREAM

Out of town they rolled and down
a big hill, picking up speed.

People ran out of their houses. They
thought a tornado was coming or that
the moon had fallen. Cars and trucks
stopped on the road, and the drivers dived
into the ditches. Cows fainted. Horses ran
away. It was a sight to see.

A big truck got tangled in the Ferris wheel
and was carried along too. Fletcher didn't know
what was in the truck until a little later when
they scattered some Boy Scouts and rolled over
their campfire.

ZIP! BLAM! ZOWIE!

Then he knew what was in the truck—fireworks for the Fourth of July. Great gobs of fireworks began to blow off. The noise was frightful. Fletcher had to stuff his fingers into his ears. It was so loud you couldn't have heard a lion roar if he had been sitting next to you.

The wheel raced through a farmyard zipping rockets through the barn.

Down the side of a mountain they rolled, faster and
faster. At the bottom lay the Atlantic Ocean. Fletcher
hugged a hippopotamus sitting next to him because
hippos are very good swimmers.

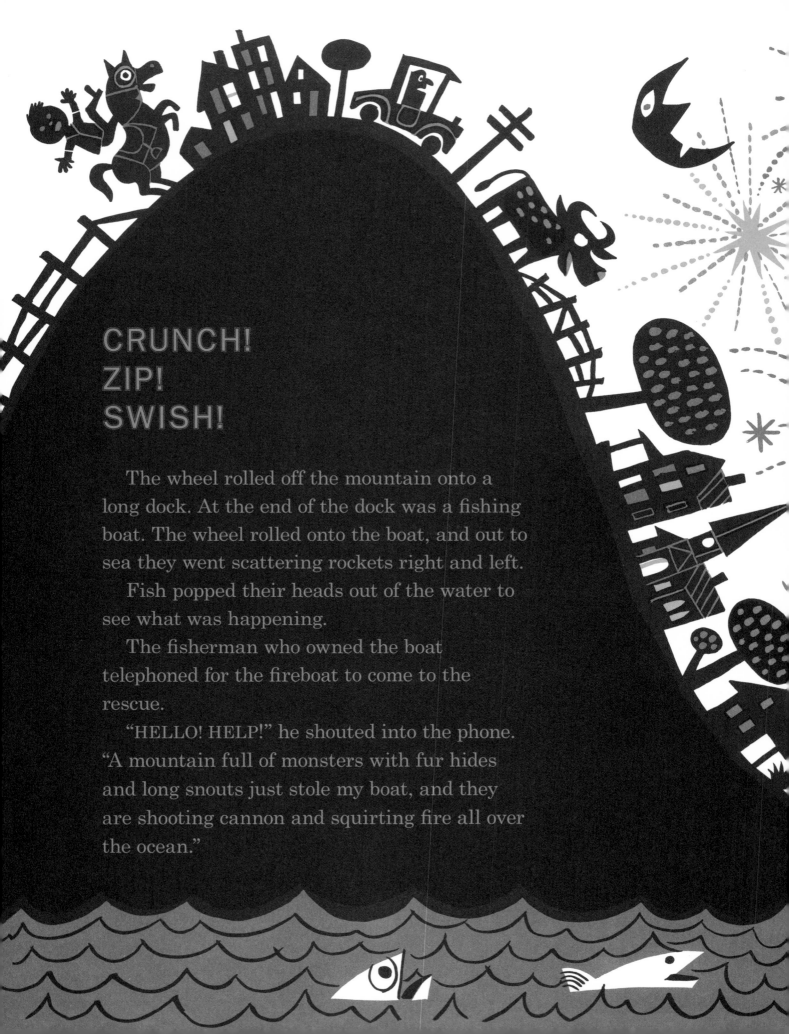

CRUNCH!
ZIP!
SWISH!

The wheel rolled off the mountain onto a long dock. At the end of the dock was a fishing boat. The wheel rolled onto the boat, and out to sea they went scattering rockets right and left.

Fish popped their heads out of the water to see what was happening.

The fisherman who owned the boat telephoned for the fireboat to come to the rescue.

"HELLO! HELP!" he shouted into the phone. "A mountain full of monsters with fur hides and long snouts just stole my boat, and they are shooting cannon and squirting fire all over the ocean."

Fletcher's floating wheel was shooting so many rockets and fireworks that the fireboat couldn't get near them at first. Finally it dashed in with all nozzles squirting and splashed water all over Fletcher and his passengers and put out the fireworks.

When the fireboat came closer, the crew saw
Fletcher all wet and cold sitting there in that big
wheel hugging a hippopotamus. They had to laugh.
They roared and howled.

Then they took Fletcher and all of the animals to shore and sent them home in trucks.

When the truck came home to our house, the driver climbed out and talked to Papa. While he talked, I could see Papa's face getting darker and darker, and I sure began to feel sorry for old Fletcher. When he finally climbed out of the truck, Papa took him by the ear.

They marched into the barn and closed the door. I guess you know what happened to Fletcher in there.

I'll bet you my best jackknife that Fletcher won't be neglecting his duties and chasing rabbits again. He learned a lesson that day. He found out that a little teeny-weeny error can grow into a whopping big mistake almost before you can say

KA-CHOW!